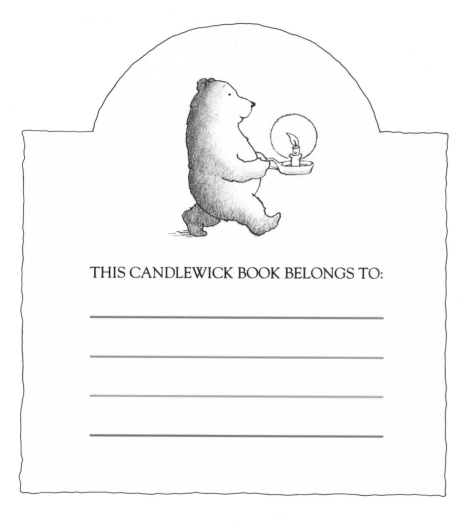

THIS CANDLEWICK BOOK BELONGS TO:

_____

_____

_____

_____

Extracts from the Authorized King James Version
of the Bible, the rights of which are vested in the
Crown in perpetuity within the United Kingdom, are
reproduced by permission of Eyre & Spottiswoode
Publishers, Her Majesty's Printers, London.

The words are taken from the Gospel
of St. Luke (chapters 1&2), the Gospel of St. Matthew
(chapter 2), and the Book of Isaiah (chapter 9).

First U.S. paperback edition 1996

Library of Congress Cataloging-in-Publication Data

Bible. N.T. Gospels. English. Authorized. Selections. 1996.
The Nativity / illustrated by Juan Wijngaard.
Originally published: New York : Lothrop, Lee & Shepard Books, 1990.
ISBN 1-56402-981-6
1. Jesus Christ—Nativity—Juvenile literature. I. Wijngaard, Juan.
BT315.A3   1996   96-14041
232.92—dc20

2 4 6 8 10 9 7 5 3

Printed in Hong Kong

The pictures in this book were done in watercolor.

Candlewick Press
2067 Massachusetts Avenue
Cambridge, Massachusetts 02140

THE NATIVITY

Illustrated by
JUAN WIJNGAARD

CANDLEWICK PRESS
CAMBRIDGE, MASSACHUSETTS

In the days of Herod, the king of Judaea, the angel Gabriel was sent from God unto a city of Galilee, named Nazareth, to a virgin espoused to a man whose name was Joseph. And the virgin's name was Mary.

THE ANGEL GABRIEL WAS SENT FROM GOD

The angel came in unto her, and said, Hail, thou that art highly favoured, the Lord is with thee: blessed art thou among women. And when she saw him, she was troubled at his saying and cast in her mind what manner of salutation this should be. The angel said unto her, Fear not, Mary: for thou hast found favour with God and behold thou shalt conceive in thy womb, and bring forth a son, and shalt call his name JESUS. He shall be great, and shall be called the Son of the Highest; and of his kingdom there shall be no end.

And Mary said, Behold the handmaid of the Lord; be it unto me according to thy word. And the angel departed from her.

"BLESSED ART THOU AMONG WOMEN"

And it came to pass in those days, that there went out a decree from Caesar Augustus, that all the world should be taxed, every one in his own city. And Joseph went up from Galilee unto the city of David, which is called Bethlehem (because he was of the house and lineage of David) to be taxed with Mary, being great with child.

JOSEPH WENT UP UNTO BETHLEHEM

And so it was, that, while they were there, the days were accomplished that she should be delivered and she brought forth her firstborn son, and wrapped him in swaddling clothes, and laid him in a manger; because there was no room for them in the inn.

SHE WRAPPED HIM IN SWADDLING CLOTHES

There were in the same country shepherds abiding in the field, keeping watch over their flock by night. And, lo, the angel of the Lord came upon them, and the glory of the Lord shone round about them: and they were sore afraid.

And the angel said unto them, Fear not: for, behold, I bring you good tidings of great joy, which shall be to all people. For unto you is born this day in the city of David a Saviour, which is Christ the Lord. And this shall be a sign unto you; Ye shall find the babe wrapped in swaddling clothes, lying in a manger.

THE GLORY OF THE LORD SHONE ROUND

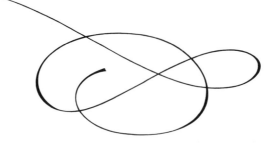

And suddenly there was with the angel a multitude of the heavenly host praising God and saying, Glory to God in the highest, and on earth peace, good will toward men.

And it came to pass, as the angels were gone away from them into heaven, the shepherds said one to another, Let us now go even unto Bethlehem, and see this thing which is come to pass, which the Lord hath made known unto us.

"GLORY TO GOD IN THE HIGHEST"

And they came with haste, and found Mary, and Joseph, and the babe lying in a manger. And when they had seen it, they made known abroad the saying which was told them concerning this child. And all they that heard it wondered at those things which were told them by the shepherds.

THEY FOUND THE BABE IN A MANGER

Now when Jesus was born, behold, there came wise men from the east to Jerusalem, saying, Where is he that is born King of the Jews? for we have seen his star in the east, and are come to worship him.

THERE CAME WISE MEN FROM THE EAST

When Herod the king had heard these things he was troubled, and all Jerusalem with him. And when he had gathered all the chief priests and scribes of the people together, he demanded of them where Christ should be born. And they said unto him, In Bethlehem of Judaea.

Then Herod, when he had privily called the wise men, sent them to Bethlehem, and said, Go and search diligently for the young child; and when ye have found him, bring me word again, that I may come and worship him also.

HEROD THE KING WAS TROUBLED

When they had heard the king, they departed; and, lo, the star, which they saw in the east, went before them, till it came and stood over where the young child was. When they saw the star, they rejoiced with exceeding great joy.

And when they were come into the house, they saw the young child with Mary his mother, and fell down, and worshipped him: and when they had opened their treasures, they presented unto him gifts; gold, and frankincense, and myrrh. And being warned of God in a dream that they should not return to Herod, they departed into their own country another way.

THEY PRESENTED UNTO HIM GIFTS

And when they were departed, behold, the angel of the Lord appeareth to Joseph in a dream, saying, Arise, and take the young child and his mother, and flee into Egypt, and be thou there until I bring thee word: for Herod will seek the young child to destroy him.

THE ANGEL APPEARETH IN A DREAM

When he arose, he took the young child and his mother by night, and departed into Egypt: and was there until the death of Herod, when they returned into Galilee, to their own city Nazareth.

FOR UNTO US A CHILD IS BORN, UNTO US A SON IS GIVEN AND THE GOVERNMENT SHALL BE UPON HIS SHOULDER AND HIS NAME SHALL BE CALLED WONDERFUL, COUNSELLER THE MIGHTY GOD, THE EVERLASTING FATHER, THE PRINCE OF PEACE.

HE TOOK THE YOUNG CHILD INTO EGYPT

JUAN WIJNGAARD is the illustrator of many books for children, including Selina Hastings's retellings of *Sir Gawain and the Green Knight* and *Sir Gawain and the Loathly Lady*. In illustrating *The Nativity*, he tried "to portray the holy family as ordinary people to whom extraordinary things happen."